To Nick...

Here's to finding your own special place in the WORLD! *

Carole Hamburger

The Star Pupil

a dot's quest to find his place in the world...

WRITTEN AND ILLUSTRATED
BY CAROLE HAMBURGER

Best Always —
Carole Hamburger

CHERRY STREET PRESS

TO ERIC AND DAVID....WITH LOVE

To be what we are, and to become
what we are capable of becoming
is the only end in life.

Robert Louis Stevenson

Your vision will become clear only when you look into your heart.
Who looks outside, dreams.
Who looks inside, awakes.

Carl Jung

Second Edition-First Printing 2008
ISBN 13: 978-0-9764921-2-2
Library of Congress: 2008930021
Copyright © 2008 Carole Hamburger
Printed and bound in Singapore

A new baby dot was born one day.

He was tiny...but perfect in every way.

His mother said, "You are my pride and joy,

Such a well-rounded dot, my darling boy."

His father said, "Son, you're much more than a dot.

You're the whole world to me in one special spot."

His parents adored him, of that he was sure.

Never before had a dot been loved more.

They taught him to talk, and walk steady and stable.

When time came for school he was ready and able.

So he went off to learn as much as he could

About all the things that he knew that he should–

Such as numbers, and letters, and music, and art.

He became a **STAR PUPIL**...he was just so smart!

Then came the day when he was all grown.
It was time to decide on a job of his own,
But he didn't have even the tiniest clue
What in the world that he wanted to do.
He needed direction – he just didn't know
Which way to turn or which way to go.

His mother said, "Son, there are so many ways
For you to spend the rest of your days.
When you finally decide how to make your mark,
You may be light or you may be dark.
You may be tiny or big as the sky,
But you'll always be a star in my eye.
And, Son, one thing more before you start...
Remember to always *follow your heart*."

His father said, "Lad, the choice has to be yours,
So just travel the road and start opening doors.
Behind one of those doors you might find the key
That unlocks the answer to what you will be.
The quest for your calling may be fast or slow.
It's not always easy to find, but I know
Whatever you choose you will shine...you'll go far.
Just always remember to *be who you are*."

Each word that they said had been caring and wise.
He hugged them and then he said his 'Goodbyes.'
It was hard leaving home, but he couldn't stay.
He knew it was time to find his own way.

There are so many choices and so many ways
For me to spend the rest of my days.
But with so many things I can choose to be...
I must find the best job that lets me be me.

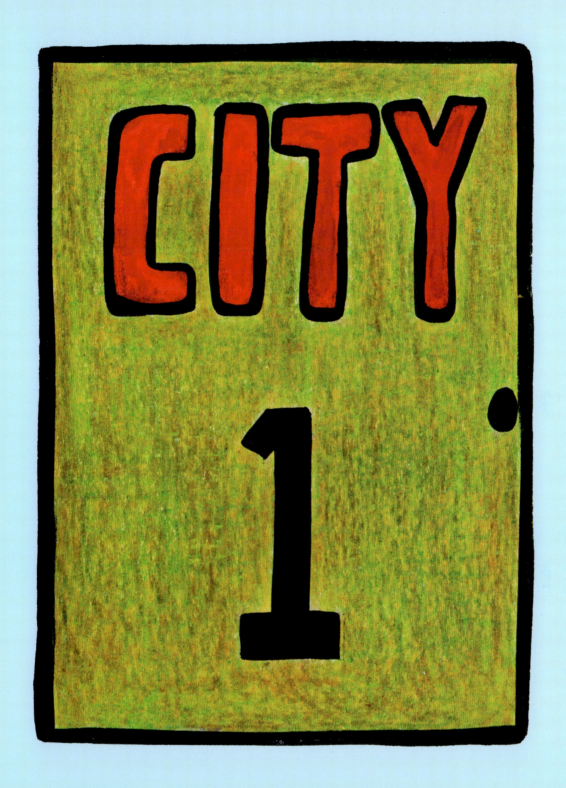

Then he went off to see the world so new.

To find the right job – something special to do.

The road led to Doorway Number One.

It said **CITY** across it...his search had begun!

When he opened the door he was filled with awe

From the sounds that he heard and the sights that he saw.

The sidewalks were flooded with folks-on-the-go.

The skyscrapers stretched high above streets below.

So much hustle and bustle – such towering height!

Dashing crowds in the day – flashing lights in the night.

He searched the whole city and when he was through

There were so many things that he knew he could do.

He could work in time management
On watches or clocks.
That would keep him so busy
Since time never stops.

He could be a decimal point
In the world of finance.
That might bring him prestige
If he gave it a chance.

And working on contracts
Could really be fine
When folks sign on his part
Of the dotted line...

Or maybe a button
Is what he should be.
There are buttons used
Everywhere in the city.
Some buttons have numbers,
Some buttons have signs,
Some buttons have words,
And some buttons have lines.

What a selection the city provided!
But with some reflection he finally decided
Though each job was exciting and easy to find,
He had to move on...he had made up his mind.

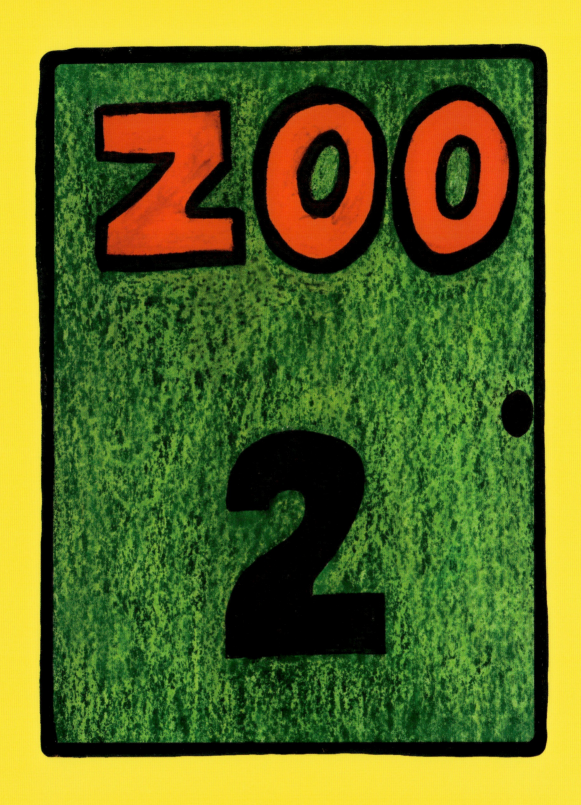

He followed the road and found Door Number Two.

The three letters near the top spelled the word **ZOO**.

When he entered this door his eyes opened wide.

Mother Nature was waiting to be his guide!

She ushered him in with her natural grace

And gave him a tour of this beautiful place.

Then she whispered encouragement into his ear.

"I have wonderful jobs for you in here.

Dots give the world such visual pleasures.

You could be one of my many treasures.

Would you like to be part of an animal's hide?

That's a job that could make you swell with pride."

But before he could answer
A girl skipped close by–
A giggling girl with a
Gleam in her eye.
He saw freckles all speckled
Across her nose
And he wondered...

As the girl skipped away he felt a light breeze
That caused a slight tickle across his knees.
He looked down and saw flowers – each one with a dot.
Another job giving him reason for thought.

When the sun disappeared and the day grew late,
The zookeeper started to lock up the gate.
So he thanked Mother Nature for being his guide.
It was tempting to stay, but he knew deep inside
He needed to find other doors to go through–
Other places to see, other dot-jobs to do.

The zoo is a fabulous place to be
But it might be a bit TOO CONFINING for me.
Something's calling to me, but I'm not sure
What it is...so I'll search some more.

14

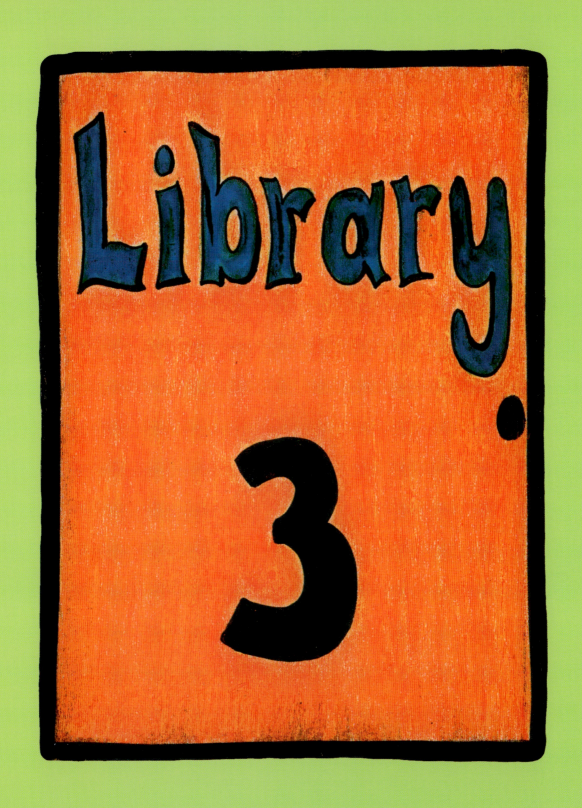

He got back on the road and found Door Number Three.
The letters on this door spelled **LIBRARY**.

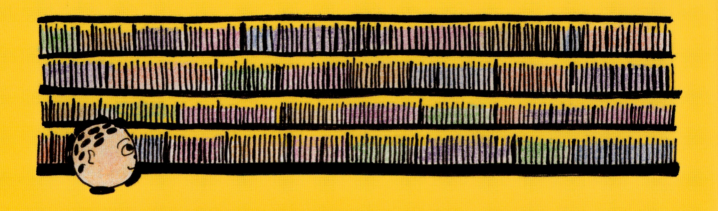

When he walked in and carefully looked all around,
He found hundreds of books but heard hardly a sound.
The number of volumes before his eyes
Suddenly made him realize...

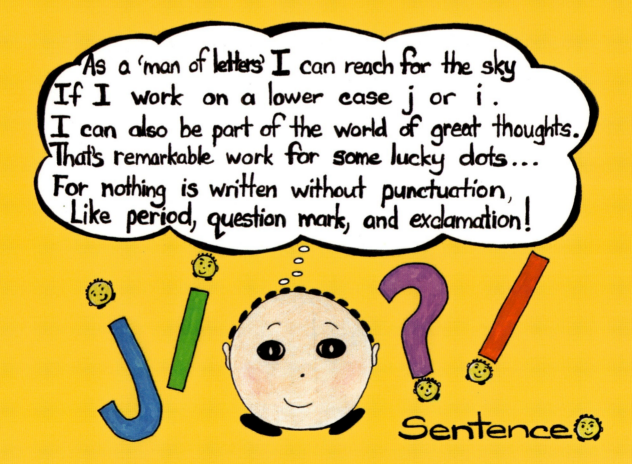

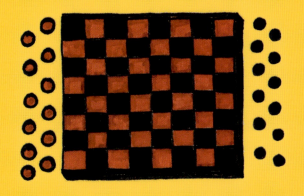

Close to the shelves
Where the books were stored
He discovered a
Red and black checker board.
The checkers were resting
Until the next game.
Would this be the job to bring
Honor and fame?

If I were a checker I could Jump and compete. I might get to Be **KING!** That would really be neat.

Next, he saw a computer
Perched on a shelf
And he instantly started to
Think to himself...

Star Pupil
Com

Maybe computer work would be The best. I'd be the **DOT** in a **DOT-com** Address.

Dot
to
Dot
Activity
Book

Then a book of activities caught his eye.
This got him excited because he could try
Being the star in his very own book!
So he turned the page to take a look.

He loved everything in the library.

It was almost as perfect as it could be–

Except for the fact there was so little noise.

He heard hardly a sound from the girls and boys.

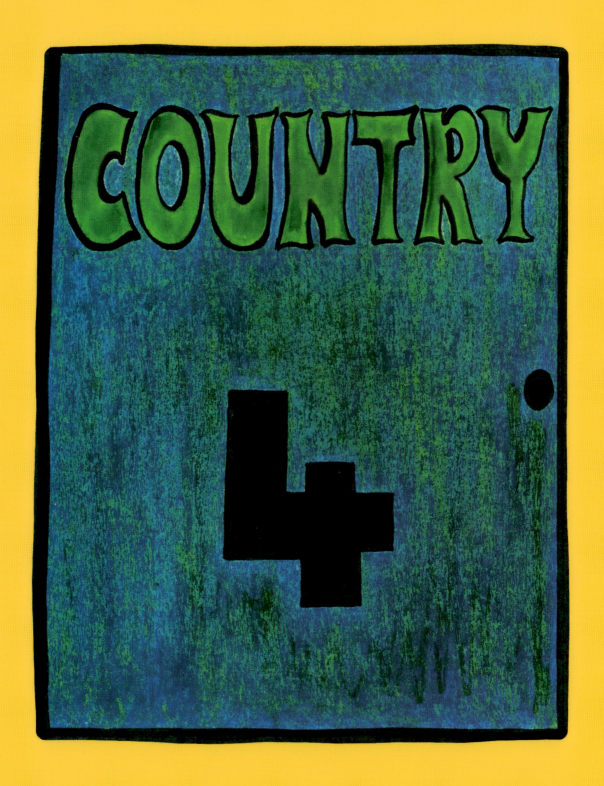

He knew it was time for the road once more

So he traveled until he found Door Number Four.

Written across it as clear as could be

Were the letters that spelled out the word **COUNTRY**.

Opening that door brought a breath of fresh air,
And to his surprise they were having a fair!
The fairgrounds were bursting with laughter and song,
Dazzling shows, bright balloons, and rides racing along.
All the sights and the sounds made him giddy that day—
For he sensed something special was coming his way!

The tune that he heard gave him the idea
That music could be a rewarding career.

As he walked on he came upon art in a frame.
It beckoned to him as if calling his name.

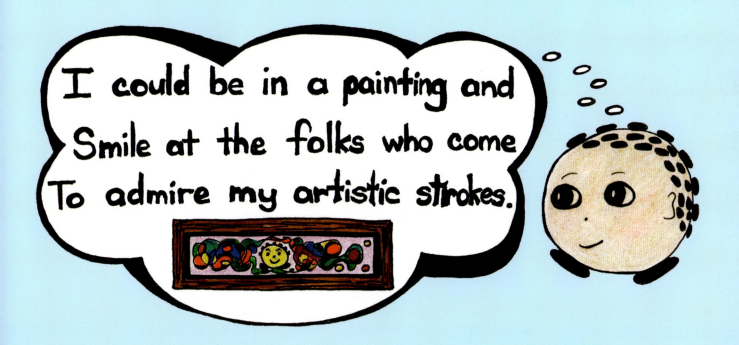

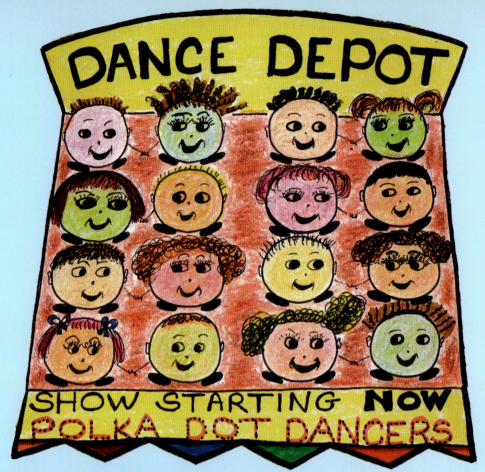

While he considered both music and art

He watched as the dancers got off to a start.

There were colorful polka-dots lined up in rows

Looking happy and free as they twirled on their toes.

They were dancing the polka and whirling about.

His heart was now pounding...he wanted to SHOUT!

At the end of the show he heard squeals of delight
And loud laughter from children suspended in flight
As they soared through the air on the carnival rides.
Some rides swirled in circles, some bumped side-to-side.
The sounds of excitement and joy made him run
Just as fast as he could to join in the fun.

But, as he rushed toward the rides he found one more door.

A small one – not like the doors opened before.

The letters on this door spelled **ROCKET RIDE**,

So he opened it up and he went inside.

24

He fastened each button, buckle, and snap,

Which tightened the straps on his shoulders and lap.

Then he blasted off to outer space

Where the stars were twinkling close to his face.

Was this a sign from up above?

Would a shining star be the work he would love?

Then off in the distance he spied a dot.

It was spinning around in a heavenly spot

With colors of blue, and brown, and green—

The most *awesome* sight he had ever seen!

For right there in full view was a magical place.

It was Planet Earth traveling through time and through space.

Yet the far-away world seemed so fragile and small.

How could one tiny dot really matter at all?

But it mattered so much! He *had* to go home,
Back to the family and friends he had known–
Back to the place where the girls and boys
Make that incredibly happy noise.

Now I know what I am after...
I need to hear the children's laughter!

And suddenly it was as clear as the sky.

His long search was over – and now he knew why.

This time he had opened *his own private door*–

The door deep inside that he couldn't ignore.

Yes, the answer had been with him right from the start...

Hiding behind the door to **HIS HEART**.

At last I know what was calling to me.
It was there all along, but too close to see.
I'll be the **STAR PUPIL** that shines in the
Eyes of all the world's children
So they'll realize . . .

In this journey called Life that is given to you

There are roads to be taken and doors to go through.

Each day brings exciting new things to see.

Adventures await, and there always will be

So many choices and so many ways

For you to spend the rest of your days.

With all of the wonderful things you can do

NOW IT'S YOUR TURN TO FIND

WHAT IS CALLING TO YOU.

*   *   *

Once you do this you can always be true

To the path that you follow...and the star inside YOU!